our generation

This is Everly's story.

EVERLY ™

A LOVE OF BOWLING

BY

SUSAN HUGHES

ILLUSTRATED BY GÉRALDINE CHARETTE

An Our Generation® *book*

MAISON BATTAT INC. *Publisher*

Thank you to the Battat editorial team for their help in creating this book, especially editor Joanne Burke Casey and designer Véronique Chartrand.

Read all the adventures in the
Our Generation® Book Series

Read more about **Our Generation®** books and dolls online:
www.ogdolls.com

CONTENTS

EXTRA! EXTRA! READ ALL ABOUT IT!

*Big words, wacky words, powerful words, funny words...
what do they all mean? They are marked with this symbol *.
Look them up in the Glossary at the end of this book.*

Chapter One

RUNNING A BIT LATE

"Almost ready to head out, girls?" I heard my dad calling from upstairs. "Your mom and I are just grabbing our bowling bags."

"Yup!" The voices of my sisters, Nancy and Monica, came from the family room.

"And you, Everly?" That was Mom's voice, also from upstairs.

"I'm almost ready!" I called back. I was at the front door, with my bowling bag, pulling on my black-and-pink boots.

My family always seems to run a bit late. We're constantly telling each other to hurry up so we can get to places on time.

But today it was even more important to be on time. It was our family reunion* bowling tournament*. Every year it's held on the first weekend in January, and I had been looking forward to it for months.

Mom is a pretty good bowler because she's bowled since she was a kid. Same with Dad, and their brothers and sisters, who are my uncles and aunts. A love of bowling seems to run in our family!

My oldest sister, Nancy, came hurrying toward the front hallway, holding her bowling bag in one hand and buttoning her coat with the other hand. She's 13 years old and a member of the teen bowling league* at Let it Roll! Bowling Alley.

That's the alley* in our town, Huntsford, where all of our family bowls and where we always have our family tournaments. Nancy practices with her team every single week, which is why she's so good.

My younger sister, Monica, came thumping along behind her. She's only five years old, but she likes bowling, too. She holds the ball with two hands and pushes it along to get it to roll all the way down the alley.

And me? I'm eight, and I'm still a beginner, too, but I really want to get better.

Mom and Dad have given me some tips and we bowl together on weekends quite a bit. Plus, I've watched almost all of Nancy's practices and league games. That's how I've been trying to learn. I've never had formal bowling lessons.

While Nancy grabbed a hat, I helped Monica button up her jacket and put on her favorite animal-print boots.

I have my own bright yellow bowling ball and sparkly blue bag, but I've never had my own brand-new pair of bowling shoes.

"I wish I didn't have to keep wearing all your old shoes, Nancy," I complained. "I'm sure I'd bowl better with my very own shoes."

"Not until your feet stop growing!" Mom said, as she and Dad came down the stairs.

"That was the rule in my house when I was growing up, too," Dad added.

We all jumped into the car and buckled up for the 15-minute drive to the bowling alley. The

whole way, as I looked out at the falling snow, I was thinking about what an amazing bowler Nancy is. I wish I were as good she is.

Nancy always tells me that I'm doing fine and that I'm as good as she was when she was my age. But I'm pretty sure she's just trying to be nice.

"I hope I do well today!" I said softly, but I guess Mom heard me.

"Now remember, honey," she said. "The whole idea of this event is to have fun with the family and enjoy the bowling!"

"*I* want to have fun!" Monica chimed in.

"Me, too!" said Nancy, giving Monica a high five*.

Nancy turned to me and gave me a high five as well. I smiled at her. I really did want to have fun, too. But I couldn't seem to stop thinking, *What if I make a mistake or do something dumb?*

Chapter Two

FAMILY REUNION

As we pulled into the parking lot, we all saw the huge "BOWL" sign on the roof of the alley. "We're here! We're here!" Monica sang out. "We're here at Let it Roll! Bowling Alley!"

My whole family loves this place. For one thing, Mom and Dad have said that they actually met in this very bowling alley way back when*. Plus, we all really like Mr. and Mrs. Manelli, who have owned the alley for a very long time.

And me, I also love the sights and sounds of this alley. I like the bright lights and the lively music that's always playing. Of course I adore the delicious smells that always seem to be wafting toward me from the snack area!

But most of all, I like the sounds of the balls crashing into the pins* and the cheering and yelling

of the bowlers. It's so exciting!

It looked like we were the last family to arrive. I spotted my ten cousins, my aunts, uncles and two of our grandparents.

"Hey there, slowpokes*! Welcome!" Dad's brother, Uncle David, called to us. "Come on over here once you've hung up your jackets and put on your bowling shoes. Except for you, Monica," he added. He knows that my little sister likes bowling in socks, without any shoes!

Other relatives greeted us as well.

Soon we all gathered around Uncle David. He told us who would be on which team. Dad, Mom, Nancy and I were each on a different team. Mom and Monica were on the same team so Mom could keep an eye on my little sister.

"You're on my team," said my cousin Winnifred, grabbing my arm. "It's us and Uncle Pete. And Gabe," she added, pointing to her brother.

As usual, each team had a cool name. Our team came up with the name "The Four

16

Tornadoes." Nancy was on a team called "Hot Shots."

I really wished that Nancy and I could be on the same team sometime. If we were both on the same team, she'd cheer for me, and that would help me do well. But playing against her? It makes me nervous. Plus I want to win, of course, and Nancy is so good! With her on our team, we'd win for sure.

The bowling began. Ten pins are set up in the shape of a triangle at the end of the lane by an automatic pinsetter*. Bowlers try to score points by knocking down as many pins as they can. Every bowler on a team has ten turns to bowl. Bowlers get two throws each turn. The team that has the most points wins.

"You're up first, Winn!" said Uncle Pete. "Do your best!"

Winn doesn't have her own ball, so she had chosen one when she got to the alley. That's what people usually do when they don't own their own ball. They choose one with finger holes that are the right size for them. They also check that the ball doesn't feel too heavy or too light.

"Go, Winn!" I cheered, along with her brother, Gabe.

Winn is older than I am. She's in middle school, and I don't know her very well. From her very first throw, I could tell that she still wasn't a great bowler. When the ball headed right into the gutter*, it didn't even seem to bother her.

It bothered Gabe, though. I heard him groan. Gabe is my age. We both go to Forest Glen Elementary School and are even in the same class. But he sort of ignores me.

Whenever our families get together, he always tries to hang out with the older kids. If he ends up being around me and the other cousins his own age, he acts like he's the boss of everyone. I've tried to be nice to him, even though he doesn't always seem to be nice to me in return.

Oh well, I thought, *the most important thing right now is that he bowls well and tries to win the game.*

18

"Hey kiddo, are you OK?" Uncle Pete asked me. "Why do you look so worried?"

"Oh!" I turned from watching Winn take her second throw. "I'm just nervous about my turn, I guess. Hey, should I keep score, Uncle Pete?" I asked.

There's an electronic scoreboard that keeps track of the scores, but I thought doing it myself might distract me and help me settle down.

"Hey, remember we're not here to win," Uncle Pete told me with a grin. "Just relax and have fun with your cousins." He's my mom's brother, and he sounds just like her!

"I'll try," I said. I looked over at Dad and saw that he was on a team with his sister (my aunt) and two of his brother's kids (my cousins).

Mom and Monica's team was on the lane next to Dad's team. They were letting Monica use a ramp* today because she's the youngest player and it helps her aim the ball. I would *never* agree to use a ramp, not ever. Nancy never used a ramp in her whole life when she was bowling, so there was no way I ever wanted to either.

But Monica didn't seem to care. My little sister likes bowling, but she doesn't take it too seriously. I've seen her get so excited about placing the bowling balls in order—by the colors of the rainbow—on the bowling ball return* that she's asked another player on her team to take her turn!

Mom flashed me a questioning look. She knows I can get a bit intense* when I bowl. I smiled back to let her know that everything was OK so far.

I looked back at Winn just as her second try knocked down three pins. She only got three points. She shrugged* and then clapped for herself, shouting, "Yes!"

Next, Gabe was up. I'm pretty sure he wanted a strike, which is when you knock down all the pins on the first throw. But his first throw wasn't that good. He only knocked down two pins.

He looked like he didn't care, but I suspected he did.

However, he knocked down the remaining eight pins on his second throw. When you knock down all the pins after the second ball, it's called a "spare." A big grin spread across his face.

"Way to go, Gabe!" Winn yelled.

"Nice one!" said Uncle Pete, as he patted him on the shoulder.

I grinned at Gabe, too. Scoring in bowling is tricky. There's a special way to keep track of how many pins are knocked down, marking Xs and lines on a score sheet.

I looked over to see if Uncle Pete was recording the score. In past family tournaments, the scorekeepers got so involved in cheering on their teams or chatting with family members that they sometimes forgot! I was about to go over and remind him.

"Evie, your turn," said Gabe, impatiently. "Come on."

Chapter Three

CATCHING THE HOT SHOTS

My hand-me-down* bowling shoes were on. I had taken my bowling ball out of my bag and carefully shined it with my cleaning towel. I always did this before I began a game. I was excited to play!

I stood in the lane well behind the foul line*. If you step over it, your throw doesn't count, no matter how good it is.

I weighed the ball in my hand and eyed the pins. I really, really wanted to do well. I'm never happy unless I do my best. But feeling like I always need to be perfect seems to make me do worse instead. It takes a bit of the fun out of bowling.

I glanced over at Nancy to see if she was watching me. I cared so much about what she would think of my game that I wasn't even sure if

I really wanted her to watch me. It depended on if I did well or not! Nope, she was laughing with her team.

I was sort of relieved. I turned my attention back to the bowling pins at the far end of the lane.

"Evie, please just go!" muttered Gabe. That made me even more nervous. I tried to ignore him and keep my attention on the lane. I took a few slow breaths, stepped to the foul line, and—

"Finally!" Gabe blurted out, just as I released the ball. Startled, I let go of the ball funny and it took off at a strange angle, sped onward, and then quickly rolled into the gutter.

I spun around. "You made me drop that!" I told Gabe. I was so upset. *Why did he do that? He's even on my team!*

"Sorry," Gabe said, looking embarrassed. "Sorry about that."

But it didn't help because I wasted my first throw and I only had one more in that turn. As I waited by the ball return for my yellow ball, I glanced up at the scoreboard. It listed all the teams.

I saw that the Hot Shots team was ahead, probably thanks to Nancy.

But I was also sure that if I started off well—if I got a spare right now—my team could do all right. We could catch the Hot Shots.

"Go on, Evie," complained Gabe again. "Take your ball and go!"

I didn't need him to rush me. I already felt enough pressure from myself!

Uncle Pete was talking casually with one of my aunts, laughing and joking. He gave me a thumb's-up but he didn't pressure me. Winn wasn't even watching.

I picked up my ball. I knew I could do well if I could only focus. But the lively music that I usually loved to hear seemed so loud now. And then Winn came over and asked me if I wanted to hear a joke, right then! I said no, but she carried on chatting anyway.

"Look, Ev," she said. "Over there. There's a birthday party of 12-year-old boys playing in those three lanes."

"Sorry, Winn. I'm trying to concentrate*," I said, trying hard to speak nicely.

Winn smiled, said OK, and then wandered away.

I looked again toward the bowling pins at the end of the lane, trying to focus. I held out the ball. I stepped to the foul line, just the way I've seen Nancy do again and again, and I got ready to release the ball—

Suddenly I realized I was standing right on the foul line. My throw wouldn't count if I let go of it. I tried to hold onto the ball and not release it, but *yikes!* It was slipping from my hands.

Oh no! I'm dropping it! I felt so frustrated that I couldn't think straight.

Forget it, I said to myself, angrily. I pulled my hands away, giving up, and just let the ball drop down onto the wooden bowling lane. It made a terrible crashing sound as it hit. It sounded just the way I felt, like everything was wrong. My ball bounced and then rolled away down the gutter.

I had ruined my score and now we'd never

25

win. I wanted to cry.

Then I realized that everyone on my team was frozen in place, staring at me. Each of them looked concerned and puzzled. I was so embarrassed. I froze in place, too.

I didn't know what to do. So I just turned and hurried away from our lane.

Chapter Four

PLANNING WITH MR. MANELLI

How could I make such a bad throw? Stepping on the foul line? Losing my points? We'd never win now.

I looked up. Somehow I had ended up next to the snack area. I stood there, trying not to cry.

Mr. and Mrs. Manelli were coming toward me. Mrs. Manelli gave me a gentle smile as she passed by. But Mr. Manelli came over and just stood near me, quietly. I didn't feel like talking yet and he seemed to sense that.

Dad began to head over, but when he saw Mr. Manelli was with me, he stopped, nodded and hung back.

For a few moments, Mr. Manelli and I didn't speak. Then I swallowed a few times and dabbed at my eyes. I started to feel a little calmer.

Mr. Manelli began to talk. He told me that he saw what happened.

"I think you were trying to do your best, Ev, like always," he said. "But you made a mistake and you felt frustrated. Is that right?"

"I stepped on the foul line," I said. "That's something a beginner does. What if Nancy saw? It made us get zero points for my turn. So for sure, we'll lose now."

I took a deep breath. I looked at the toes of my shoes. "I'm sorry for letting the ball hit the lane so hard," I said.

While Mr. Manelli appeared to be thinking for a moment, Dad came over. He and I waited to hear what Mr. Manelli would say.

"I accept your apology," he said. "But listen, Everly. How about you spend some time here at Let it Roll! over the next few months? You could help me out with some tasks. And maybe I can help you improve your bowling skills."

"Really?" I cried, surprised. "Thank you! Is that OK with you and Mom, Dad?"

"Everly can certainly come and help you out," Dad said. "That's a good idea. She can come on the nights that I drop off Nancy for her league practices, if that's alright with you, Mr. Manelli."

Dad frowned. "But the coaching won't be necessary. That's too much trouble for you."

Mr. Manelli shook his head. "Not at all. I've been friends with you and Everly's mom since… well, since forever! In fact, I still remember the day you two met here at the alley."

Mr. Manelli looked at me and said, "One day I'll tell you that story."

Then he put his hand on Dad's shoulder. "I'd enjoy having Everly help me out. I'd also enjoy teaching her a little of what I know about bowling."

"Please, Dad?" I begged. "Is it OK?"

Dad went to have a quick discussion with Mom and I could see her nodding enthusiastically while they talked.

Dad soon returned and said Mom thought it was a great idea. So Dad, Mr. Manelli and I made plans for me to come along to the alley with Nancy the very next week.

Chapter Five

FINDING THE FUN!

It was Thursday night—four days after the family reunion. Nancy and I were back at the bowling alley. I was watching her practice with her team. *I wish I could be bowling right now and not just waiting to help out,* I thought.

Then Mr. Manelli called me over to the bowlers' seating area a few lanes away. When he asked me if I wanted to start with a lesson, I smiled. And I agreed, of course.

Mr. Manelli told me that I probably already knew lots of what he would show me, but he thought it would be a good idea to review the basic techniques* with me. He began by showing me how to hold the ball properly. Next, he demonstrated* the proper arm swing for throwing the ball.

I did my best to follow his instructions. Mom and Dad have shown me how to throw, and I've copied Nancy, too. But Mr. Manelli corrected me a little, showing me how to adjust* my throw.

I tried to make the adjustments. But the arm swing wasn't quite right. I could tell.

"Good, Everly," said Mr. Manelli. "You're doing fine." But I knew I wasn't. I knew my swing wasn't perfect. Then I saw Nancy looking over at us, and I definitely didn't want her to see how badly I was doing.

"I'd like to stop now," I told Mr. Manelli, abruptly.

"All right," he said, looking surprised and a bit disappointed.

"Come along with me to the counter where we keep the rental shoes," he said. "Lots of people rent bowling shoes when they come to bowl. After they return them, they need to be sorted into men's or women's—and by size.

"When it's busy here, Mrs. Manelli and I don't always have time to put them back in the

34

proper slots where they belong. That's a job we leave for times like now, when things are slower."

"Sure," I said. "I understand."

I got to work right away. Mrs. Manelli waved Mr. Manelli over to the snack area and he stayed there, talking with her, for a while. I went as fast as I could to show Mr. Manelli that I was trying really hard.

But when he joined me again, he stopped me.

"Hang on, Everly," he said. "Look, this pair isn't in the correct place. This one isn't either." He pulled out two pairs.

Ugh! I felt like throwing the shoes on the floor. I guess I started scowling*, because Mr. Manelli asked me why I looked upset.

"I'm trying to do well, but I'm messing it up," I grumbled. "I hate it when I don't do my best."

"Listen, Everly, why don't you slow down a bit? Whether you do this job quickly or not isn't important to me," Mr. Manelli said. He smiled.

"What's important is that the shoes end up in the right place so they're easy for us to find when someone needs them."

"OK," I said.

"But there are two other really important things about doing a task," he went on. "One: Keep going until you're done with the task, even if doing it isn't fun. That's called perseverance. And two: If you can, find a way to have fun while you do it!"

"Fun?" I said, doubtfully, looking at the slots full of shoes.

"If I hurry through a job just so I can get on to the next thing, that's no good." He grinned. "I try to find the fun in everything I do, even things that seem boring!"

Mrs. Manelli was sweeping the floor nearby. "It's true," she agreed. "This man somehow manages to make the dullest things exciting. It's quite a talent he has!"

"But how can anyone make this fun?" I asked. "Not that it's so bad," I added hastily, "but

I wouldn't exactly call it exciting."

Mr. Manelli handed me the shoes that had been put in the wrong place.

"Well," he explained, "sometimes when I'm sorting bowling shoes, I tell myself stories or make up poems and limericks*."

That made me smile. "I like limericks! Can you please make one up right now?" I begged.

He chuckled. "Let's do the sorting together and I'll try."

We resumed* working together. I sorted more slowly and carefully, as Mr. Manelli had suggested. I also decided to try to make up a limerick, too.

Before I knew it, Mr. Manelli said, "OK, I've got one. Ready?" He recited:

"There once was a bowler named Fred
Who insisted he stand on his head
When he aimed for the pins
He hit the garbage bins
That upside-down bowler named Fred."

37

"That's great!" I said, giggling. "Can you make up another one?"

"Ah, but it's your turn," he told me.

"OK, but mine isn't as good as yours," I warned him.

"There once was a young girl named Allie
Who loved to go bowling at the alley
She had hand-me-down shoes
But they always made her lose
That sad young girl named Allie."

Mr. Manelli laughed and laughed. "I like it!" he exclaimed.

"Let's each think up one more," I suggested.

But all the shoes were sorted. And Nancy was calling my name, saying Mom was here to pick us up. I was actually a little disappointed. I guess sorting shoes had ended up being fun after all!

"See you next week, Mr. Manelli!" I said, and off I went.

Chapter Six

THE POINT OF PRACTICING

One week later, I was back at the bowling alley. Even though making up limericks while we worked was fun, I was a bit nervous. My last lesson hadn't gone so well. I had given up when I got frustrated.

"Hi, Everly," Mr. Manelli greeted me.

I smiled and waited. I was worried that he wouldn't want to give me another lesson, but I was too afraid to tell him that.

But right away, he said, "So, let's get started with the lesson."

I was relieved. He was going to give me another chance.

We headed toward one of the lanes. "But this time," he added, "if you feel like things aren't going well, just tell me. Then we can stop if you want."

He looked at me. "Or we can agree that you don't have to be exactly perfect at everything right away. That the whole point of practicing is doing it not-so-well a few times and then improving."

"It's a deal," I said. I knew he was right. I knew it was a good idea. I just didn't know if I could actually do that—be OK about taking my time to improve.

"So, let me show you a good throwing technique again," Mr. Manelli suggested. "Here are the three parts of a throw. Reach back. That's the beginning of the arm swing," he said, as he demonstrated.

"Swing your arm forward, keeping it close to your body." He showed me in slow motion*.

"And then here, release the ball at a low level. Don't let it bounce."

I winced* when he said that. It reminded me of dropping the ball at the family reunion.

"Reach back, arm close to body and release low." I repeated his instructions, to show him that

I was following along.

He asked me to practice the movement without a ball, and I did. Then he asked me to try it while I held my bowling ball, and I did.

Next, Mr. Manelli had me throw the ball, trying to repeat the technique.

The first two times, I didn't do it well.

I got mad at myself and frowned. "I think I want to stop," I told Mr. Manelli.

"Really? You're sure?" he asked. "Well, think of it this way. It's good that your first two throws were so bad, because now even a slightly better throw will mean you're improving!"

I had to laugh. He was right, in a funny way. So I decided to try some more throws.

I didn't get them quite perfect either, but they were a little better. And Mr. Manelli was right. I felt better because I improved. And because I didn't give in to my frustration and quit!

Chapter Seven

ANGRY WORDS

It was getting close to the end of February, and it had been snowing all month. I'd had two more bowling lessons, one week after another. Each time I had improved a bit, which made me happy.

Today, Dad had dropped Nancy and me at Let It Roll! Bowling Alley, and as soon as Mr. Manelli saw me, he motioned for me to come over to the snack area.

"I'm sorry, Everly," he said, "but we won't be able to start your lesson right away. A birthday party was booked for this afternoon, and all 20 kids have arrived at once! I need your help getting bowling shoes for each party guest."

While Mr. Manelli and I helped with the shoes, Mrs. Manelli showed the parents where they could store the birthday cake. Then she helped them decorate the snack area with balloons and streamers.

Soon the three of us had the party all set up, and the guests were bowling happily.

"Thanks, Everly," Mr. Manelli said, with a smile. "You were a big help! Now, let's head over to an empty alley. I want to teach you something new."

Mr. Manelli began working with me on my approach*. He suggested that I should always try to begin my approach in the same place and end up throwing with a consistent* arm swing.

He explained why doing the same thing each time would help me to be a better bowler. We also talked about how many steps to take during my throw.

"Now, I'd like you to practice this a few times," he said.

I tried it several times and had a little trouble, as usual. I knew I wasn't doing my best. And the kids at the birthday party were making so much noise. And the music in the bowling alley was turned up so loud.

"Let's take a break, Everly," Mr. Manelli said. Like always, he seemed to understand how I was feeling almost before I did. *How does he do that?* I wondered.

He asked me to set my ball on the ball return for a moment. When he asked, "How are you feeling right now?" I decided to be honest. I admitted that I was feeling frustrated and nervous.

"Good," he declared.

"Good?" I repeated, surprised.

He nodded. "Like most sports, bowling involves the body *and* the mind, so it's good if you can identify how your body is feeling and what emotions you're feeling.

"If you can notice how your body and mind are reacting to a situation, it can help you to control them." He paused. Then he asked, "Do you want to try something?"

"Um. OK," I replied.

"Instead of becoming frustrated and letting

46

that feeling control how you react, try to be more aware of when the feeling is starting," said Mr. Manelli. "When you feel it starting, you can stop and take a deep breath. *You* can decide how you want to act."

"Sure, I'll try that," I agreed, a bit more enthusiastically. "Thanks."

I liked his idea. I'd like to be able to stay calm even when I feel upset.

I looked curiously at Mr. Manelli. *How does he know so much about this?* I wondered. *I can't imagine him ever reacting too quickly or without thinking.*

"Advice from this old guy is now over!" announced Mr. Manelli. He suggested that I go get the ball and begin practicing again.

I did, and I didn't have to wait very long before I knew that I was starting to feel frustrated. But now I had an action plan. So I stopped and took a breath. And it wasn't easy, but I decided I wasn't going to scowl or frown or throw the ball or quit. Instead I was going to try three more throws and then stop.

I took one throw and it wasn't very good. But I didn't give up, even though the kids at the party were still noisy and the music was still loud. I tried to stay relaxed as I did two more throws. And trying to stay relaxed seemed to help, because the throws were a little bit better!

Mr. Manelli and I walked over to the snack area to get a cold drink. It was almost dinnertime, and usually the delicious smells of the hot dogs, pizza and fresh pretzels would be distracting to me. But not right now. I really wanted to find a way to tell Mr. Manelli how much his tips were helping me.

"Mr. Manelli, thanks for your help. Not just with my bowling…" I started to say, awkwardly.

"It's OK, Everly," said Mr. Manelli. "I know how it feels to get angry and act without thinking. I'm sorry to say that I've learned about this from personal experience. Let me tell you a story about

my older brother, Vince, and me."

Suddenly Mr. Manelli looked sad. He told me about growing up with his brother, and how much he loved him and had wanted Vince to be proud of him.

"I felt like I had to prove to him how good I was at everything," Mr. Manelli explained. "When we got older, Vince built up a successful business. I was happy for him. I couldn't find the right job for myself though. Over the years I worked at this and that. But nothing felt right.

"Then I got the idea to buy a bowling alley—and suddenly everything fell into place! I knew this was my dream job. I couldn't wait to show this place to Vince. And Vince did come by and congratulate me. I could see he was happy for me."

Mr. Manelli paused. "At first, my brother would try to give me lots of business tips, but I was too proud to listen. I was sure he thought I couldn't do this on my own.

"Finally one day, I told him I didn't need his

help," Mr. Manelli said, quietly. "He looked upset, but I didn't stop to think about his feelings. Instead I said some angry words to him, and then he said some angry words back. We haven't spoken to each other since."

"Oh, no!" I murmured. I couldn't believe it!

"That was quite a while ago, and I'm still upset at myself," Mr. Manelli said. "If only I hadn't reacted that way. If only I'd been in more control of myself that might never have happened."

Mr. Manelli stood quietly for a moment, sipping his cherry cola. I thought about how much I care about my own sisters—both of them—and I knew how bad Mr. Manelli must feel.

It was hard to believe that his brother wouldn't want to be his friend now.

All I could think of to say was, "I'm so sorry!" Mr. Manelli had been so kind to me. I wondered, *Is there anything I can do to help him with this problem? Anything at all?*

Chapter Eight

TAKING A BREATH

Today, everyone in my class, including me, was excited to go out for morning recess. It was the end of March, and the snow was almost gone. It actually felt like spring!

I was excited for other reasons, too. I'd had three more bowling lessons with Mr. Manelli and I've been improving. Even though my bowling isn't always perfect, I'm enjoying the practices more and more.

And I've finally started to realize that I like working alongside Mr. Manelli at the bowling alley. We always find ways to make the tasks fun.

Out in the schoolyard, some of my friends pulled out their jump ropes for the first time in months. Then we saw Gabe and his friends begin to kick a soccer ball around. Immediately, my friend Laura decided that we were going to challenge them to a game.

But I didn't really want to play soccer. I wasn't even wearing my running shoes. I wouldn't be able to run properly or play my best.

I told Laura, but she said, "Who cares? Come on, Everly!"

"I don't think so..." I started to say.

But my friends laughed and pulled on my arm. "But we need you! We want you to come and play with us!"

So I changed my mind. *Maybe it'll be fine,* I thought.

We played for a while, and it wasn't too bad. Gabe smiled at me when I happened to be running beside him for a few moments. And it was so wonderful to be playing outside again after such a long winter.

I had my jacket unzipped, and I'd stuck my hat and mittens in my pocket. Almost all the snow was gone, the sun was shining and the sky was blue. I really was having fun after all!

Then Lillian passed the ball to me. And I missed it.

The ball headed straight to Robert, who was on the other team, and he kicked it back in the other direction.

I was so mad at myself. *How could I miss that? It came straight to me!*

I slowed down. I could feel myself starting to frown. But then, guess what? At one time I would have stomped away in frustration, but today I just took a breath and paused, while I decided what to do.

And I made up my mind. Although part of me wanted to quit because I had missed such an easy kick, I didn't.

Nope, I kept on playing!

On the weekend, Mom had a bowling match with friends, so she took me along with her to the bowling alley.

Mr. Manelli reviewed with me how to let

go of the ball when it was near my ankle during the arm swing. We watched Mom and her friends play, and Mr. Manelli pointed out how well they were throwing. Then he let me try.

He didn't seem as happy as usual. I wondered if he was thinking about his brother.

I wished I could think of something to do to cheer him up. Then I recalled how happy he is when he's making up limericks and telling me stories. So when my lessons were done and we were sorting bowling shoes together, I asked him to tell me a story.

He told me he was proud of me for being so persistent with my lessons and said it reminded him of starting up the bowling alley.

"I refused to take advice from my brother," he said, "but only because I was stubborn. In reality, I didn't have any experience running a business, and neither did Mrs. Manelli! We worked hard and just kept at it.

"For a while, we didn't know if the bowling alley was going to survive, but my wife and I refused to give up. That's perseverance, right? We stuck it out, even if though it was difficult." Mr. Manelli smiled.

"After a year or two, some bowlers became regulars*. More and more people began to come and play here. We continued to persevere and then suddenly—Let it Roll! Bowling Alley became the popular place to bowl!"

I clapped my hands. "Thanks for the story," I said.

For a moment, I thought about asking Mr. Manelli about his brother. I wanted to ask if he had ever tried to get in touch with him. I wanted to see if there was anything I could do to help. But then I changed my mind. I really didn't want to ruin the nice moment! It felt so good to see Mr. Manelli smiling.

Chapter Nine

A LOVE STORY

"Look, Ev," said Nancy. She and I had just jumped out of the car and said goodbye to Dad. "The flowers outside Let it Roll! are starting to bloom!"

We admired the tiny little shoots breaking through the soil before we hurried inside. Nancy headed to her league practice, and I met up with Mr. Manelli for a lesson. Afterwards I helped do some sweeping and polishing.

An hour and a half later, Mr. Manelli and I had finished up our tasks, and Nancy was done with her practice.

"Mom won't be here for another 15 minutes or so," I told Mr. Manelli. "Remember you promised to tell us the story about how our parents met here at the bowling alley?"

"Oh, yes!" said Nancy, excitedly. "Will you tell it to us both now?"

"Sure," said Mr. Manelli. "I'd love to tell you that happy love story!"

The three of us sat down in one of the bowlers' seating areas that wasn't being used and Mr. Manelli began.

"When your parents were young, they were each on different teams in a bowling league. The teams began practicing at this alley right after we opened! Mrs. Manelli and I knew both of your parents. But they practiced on different days, so your mom and dad had never met each other.

"One weekend we had a tournament here, and on the very first evening, their two teams ended up playing against each other," continued Mr. Manelli.

"Your mom and dad were so competitive*. During the game, the other people on their teams were joking and being friendly with one another, but not your parents. They wouldn't even talk to the players on the other teams!"

"Wow, that is so *not* like the Mom and Dad I know!" exclaimed Nancy.

"Me either!" I said.

"When the game was over, almost everyone headed out. But your mom had trouble in the parking lot. She couldn't start her car. She came back in to ask me for help," said Mr. Manelli.

"I saw your dad was still there. I thought, *Here's my chance to get the ball rolling!*

"I pretended I was busy with a customer. I asked your dad if he would go and help your mom instead of me, and your dad agreed."

Nancy and I grinned at each other.

"I peeked out my office window. I saw them get your mom's car started and then chat a bit," said Mr. Manelli.

"Your parents were here all weekend because of the tournament. I saw them talking once, then again, and then again. It turns out that they actually had lots more in common than just their love of bowling."

He leaned back in his chair. "They ended up

going on several dates, and…the rest is history!"

What a great story! As Mom drove us home, Nancy told her that Mr. Manelli had finally told us how she and Dad met.

"I'm so glad that wonderful man helped your dad and I set aside our competitiveness and actually see each other," Mom said. "We both needed a reminder that bowling wasn't just something to win, but something to enjoy."

I'm so happy that bowling brought Mom and Dad together, with Mr. Manelli's help. It's one more reason to love the sport!

The next Thursday, I was at the bowling alley again. I had been thinking and thinking about Mr. Manelli and his brother.

I finished my lesson and, while we were sweeping, I decided to ask Mr. Manelli more about it.

"After your argument with your brother," I said, "did you ever try to work things out?"

"You know, during those tough years, I thought about asking my brother for help. But…" Mr. Manelli looked sad again.

"But what?" I asked.

"Well, the day after our argument, I went over to my brother's house to apologize to him. I knocked, but he wasn't there," explained Mr. Manelli.

"So I wrote a note saying I was sorry and asking him to call me so we could talk things over. I slipped the note through his mailbox. But he never did call."

"Didn't you ever try again?" I asked.

"No," admitted Mr. Manelli. "I was too stubborn."

"And what about now?" I asked.

"Oh, no," he said, surprised. "It's too late. Far too late."

"I don't agree, Mr. Manelli," I said slowly. I looked him in the eyes. "It's never too late to try."

63

Chapter Ten

THE CLASS TAKES A VOTE

That same night, Dad was out playing his weekly game of racquetball* with Uncle David. Mom told us she was going to make breaded fish with peas and rice. It's one of our favorite meals.

"Hey!" said Nancy. "How about if Everly, Monica and I all pitch in and help you, Mom?"

"Wonderful!" said Mom. "It'll be nice to slow down a bit and have some fun."

We agreed that Nancy would help prepare the meal. She loves to dip the fish fillets* in the eggs and milk and then coat them with the bread crumbs.

Monica and I said we would set the table. She and I also made special place mats for the meal. We drew undersea scenes on four pieces of white construction paper.

As we sat down to eat, we all agreed we should do this more often: a dinner night with a theme!

I began thinking again about ways I could help Mr. Manelli. I was feeling frustrated that I couldn't come up with good ideas. But then I suddenly remembered that I could always turn to my family for help.

So as we enjoyed our meal together, I told Mom, Nancy and Monica about Mr. Manelli and his argument with his brother. I finished by saying that they haven't seen each other since the argument. Monica looked puzzled.

"But they're brothers," she said.

"Yes, honey," said Mom. "I know it's hard to understand."

"It sure is," agreed Nancy.

"Mom, what can we do to help?" I asked. "There has to be something! Mr. Manelli told me that he'd like to see his brother, but he thinks it's too late to apologize now. Maybe we could try to find Vince and tell him how sorry Mr. Manelli is about what happened."

"Good idea, Ev," said Nancy. "Can we, Mom?"

"What do you think, Mom?" I asked. "Is it ever too late to say sorry?"

"No, definitely not," she said, without hesitating. "But I don't think we can speak to Mr. Manelli's brother without checking with Mr. Manelli first. We need his approval.

"Your dad and I will both speak to Mr. Manelli in person about how we all want to help, and see what he thinks. It's really nice that you care so much, Everly," she said.

The next morning, my teacher, Mr. Penn, stood at the front of the room. After he asked us to put away our math books, he told us he had something to discuss.

"It's now May, and school ends in a month," he said. "It's time to plan our end-of-the-year party. Does anyone have an idea of what we should do?"

Patrick's hand shot up. "Bowling!" he suggested. "My cousin had a bowling birthday party last year at Let it Roll! Bowling Alley. It was so much fun!"

"Yes, let's go bowling!" called out many of my classmates.

Right away, I had mixed feelings*. It might be great to go bowling with my whole class at Let it Roll! Bowling Alley. I could show everyone around. I could help with the scoring and even surprise my friends with how well I bowl!

But what if I make dumb mistakes? I worried. *What if all my balls go into the gutter? What if I don't do my best?*

Mr. Manelli had taught me that it's OK if I'm not perfect. *But can I actually count on myself to relax at the party and just have fun?*

"Any other ideas?" Mr. Penn asked.

Leanne suggested going to the indoor trampoline park and Carter suggested going roller-skating. Lots of the other kids liked those ideas, and Gabe seemed excited, too.

"Chat with one another for a moment about this and then we'll vote," said Mr. Penn.

I still wasn't sure which way I'd vote. Then suddenly, Gabe was standing right beside me!

"Ev," he said, "I just want to tell you that lately, when I've run into you at Let it Roll!, I've noticed how much you've … changed since the family reunion bowling tournament. You seem more relaxed when you bowl. It looks like it's more fun for you now."

Gabe smiled. "So I'm pretty sure you're going to vote for the bowling, but I just wanted to check. I don't want to vote for it unless you're OK with that."

I couldn't believe it! My cousin is such a cool guy. Grinning like crazy, I said, "Yes, I'm definitely voting for the bowling."

"Oh, good! Then I'll do that, too!" he said, with a thumbs-up.

When it was time for the vote, both Gabe and I put our hands up for the bowling and so did almost everyone else in our class. The bowling option won by a landslide*!

Later that night, Dad and Mom came into my bedroom to say goodnight.

"I almost forgot!" Mom said, handing me a shoebox.

"We wanted to give you these," said Dad, "because of everything you've been doing at the bowling alley."

Dad gave me a wink, and I knew he meant how I was helping out Mr. Manelli and how much better I've been doing at having fun with my bowling.

Holding my breath, I whipped off the lid and—

"New bowling shoes!" I cried. "Oh, wow! Just what I wanted! Thanks, Mom and Dad!"

I jumped up and hugged both of them. What a great surprise!

Chapter Eleven

FIRST STRIKE!

"Nice bowling shoes!" said Mr. Manelli. "Very snazzy*!"

"I'm trying to break in my shoes before our class bowling party," I explained. "It's only a few weeks away."

It was Saturday now, and Mom, Dad, my sisters and I were all at the alley, having a family-bowling afternoon.

It was so much fun bowling with them, but I couldn't focus. Mom and Dad were planning to talk to Mr. Manelli when we were done. They were going to ask him if there was some way we could help him reunite* with his brother.

Soon, Mom put down her bowling ball. "I'm a bit distracted," she said. "We *all* seem to be! So how about we take a break from the bowling and your dad and I have that chat with Mr. Manelli right now?"

"Good idea," Nancy and I said, as Monica nodded.

As Mom and Dad began their conversation with Mr. Manelli, my sisters and I tried not to stare. But to our surprise, only a few minutes later, Mr. Manelli led my parents back over to us.

"Your parents want to talk to me about my brother, Vince, but I want you all to hear this," he explained.

"Ever since I talked to Everly about Vince, my brother has been on my mind. Talking to Everly made me realize I was so silly not to try to get in touch with him again during all these years." Mr. Manelli smiled.

"I just never had the confidence to call and apologize to him again after I dropped off my note and he didn't call me back."

He gave us a big grin. "Thank you, Everly— thanks all of you—for wanting to help me with my brother. But just two days ago, I decided to find my brother's phone number myself. I'm planning to call him up and apologize. I want to try again with him!"

I smiled, happily.

"It's never too late. Everly told me that and I agree," said Mr. Manelli, looking at me.

When we returned to our game, it was *still* hard for me to bowl because I was so excited. But I didn't mind. I didn't even want to try to calm down! Not with such exciting news.

And after I got up to take my final throw, guess what? When I least expected it, I knocked all the pins down with one ball. Yes, I bowled a strike—my very first!

What made it even more special was that my whole family and Mr. and Mrs. Manelli were there to cheer along with me!

Chapter Twelve

NEVER TOO LATE FOR SORRY

It was finally happening. My end-of-the-year class party. It was so great being at Let it Roll! Bowling Alley. It feels like home to me!

I was relaxed, bowling well and truly having fun. Sure, partly it was because my classmates were asking me for bowling tips, which meant they noticed that I was a pretty good bowler. That definitely made me happy!

And also my team, the "Rocket Launchers," was winning! Even though I knew it was a bowling party and we weren't really competing, I was still happy to be winning.

But I was trying not to let it matter *too* much. I was trying to just enjoy being with my friends. And it seemed to be working.

Then, right when the party was almost over,

something bad happened. It was my final turn to bowl. My first shot was a good one. Only four pins were left standing. I was very excited.

I had the ball in my hand and I tried to concentrate as I made my throw.

But ... *uh-oh.*

I released the ball too soon.

I couldn't believe it! The ball swerved* to the side and into the gutter. It was such a sloppy mistake. Immediately I started to get upset. I felt like I'd let myself—and my team—down.

I stared angrily at the ball. I stared angrily at the pins, too, because they were all still standing. I felt the same way I'd felt at the family reunion!

But this time, I stopped. I took a breath. And I realized how silly I was being. I realized what I was doing. I was turning something fun into something upsetting. And those pins weren't going to fall down just because I was glaring* at them!

I actually giggled at the thought. Then, when I took another breath and walked away, Gabe gave me a thumbs-up!

I was so proud of myself, even though I lost my throw and didn't get any points.

❦ ❦

Soon after, the bowling party was over.

Parents began showing up to take us all home. Then I saw Dad, Mom, Monica and Nancy standing with the Manellis, chatting. My family had come to pick me up. *Oh-no!* Nancy must have seen my terrible throw. She probably thought I was a poor bowler—

One second later, I came to my senses*. Nancy's always telling me that I'm doing well, and that I'm as good at bowling as she was when she was my age. And besides, I'm still just learning. She knows that and I do, too. I don't have to be perfect.

So after I said hi to them all, I told Mr. Manelli that it had been such a fun day. I thanked him for teaching me about perseverance. I even used the word "perseverance," one that he'd taught me! Mr. Manelli actually blushed a little bit.

"*I* should be thanking *you,*" he said.

I was confused, but he gestured at a man standing beside him, a man who looked a lot like Mr. Manelli. Even before he introduced him, I guessed who he was!

"Vince!" I said.

"Yes, this is my brother, Vince," laughed Mr. Manelli. "And Vince, this is Everly, the girl I told you about. The girl I invited you here to meet today!"

I was so surprised and happy that I couldn't even speak. Vince was here, with Mr. Manelli! They were together again.

Mr. Manelli explained that he had called Vince yesterday to apologize and during the phone call, Vince kept interrupting to apologize in return. Then Vince had driven right over to the bowling alley to see his younger brother and talk in person.

"You know what?" said Mr. Manelli. "It turns out that Vince never got the note I slipped through his door so long ago."

"All these years, I was too stubborn and

proud to make the first move and get in touch with my brother and apologize," Vince admitted, shaking his head. "I just decided my brother didn't care. What a big mistake. And then time went by and I thought it was too late to say sorry."

"I thought that, too!" said Mr. Manelli. "It took this bright young girl to help me realize that..."

"...it's never too late to say sorry!" Nancy, Monica and I chimed in together.

We were all laughing, when my teacher asked for everyone's attention. Mr. Penn made a speech, saying what an enjoyable party it had been. He announced that he was giving out three awards.

He named two students, Marco and Keltie, and awarded each of them a trophy: "Best First-Timer" and "Most Amazing Happy Dancer." We all clapped and cheered.

Mr. Penn said he had one more award to give out—and he called out the name of *my* team, the Rocket Launchers.

"I'd like to give the "Team Spirit" award to the Rocket Launchers," he said.

"Congratulations to all of you. You each deserve a trophy for showing what being a good sport* is all about. You were helpful and encouraging to everyone today. You made sure you had fun, no matter what!"

I was so excited. My teammates and I congratulated one another. Nancy rushed up and gave me a hug. "I'm so happy for you, Ev," she said.

"Well done, Everly," said Mr. Manelli, who was beaming*. "Well done, indeed."

It was my first bowling trophy ever, and I couldn't be more proud!

Glossary

Many words have more than one meaning. Here are the definitions of words marked with this symbol * (an asterisk) as they are used in this story.

adjust: *to slightly change the way something is done to make it work better*

alley: *a building in which people bowl; also, a long, narrow wooden lane within the building that is used for bowling*

approach: *the way a bowler takes steps while moving close to the spot where he or she will let go of the bowling ball*

automatic pinsetter: *a machine that sets up bowling pins after they are knocked down*

beaming: *smiling brightly*

bowling ball return: *a track between lanes on which the bowling ball is automatically rolled back to the bowler*

bowling league: *teams of bowlers that compete against one another during a season*

competitive: *wanting to be better at something than anyone else*

"came to my senses": *an expression that means you stopped being silly*

concentrate: *focus very hard on something*

consistent: *done the same way over and over again*

demonstrated: *showed*

family reunion: *a gathering of many people within the same family*

fillets: *thin pieces of boneless fish*

foul line: *the line at the beginning of the lane that a bowler cannot step on or go past*

glaring: *staring angrily*

good sport: *someone who is polite, fair and friendly, even if he or she is losing*

gutter: *a long, narrow low section along each side of a bowling lane*

hand-me-down: *clothing or shoes used by one person and then passed on to another person*

high five: *a sign of agreement or celebration when two people slap each other's palm with their hands raised in the air*

intense: *having strong feelings*

landslide: *a large number of votes for one side*

limericks: *a funny poem with 5 lines (3 long and 2 short) and a certain rhyming pattern*

mixed feelings: *having good and bad feelings at once*

pins: *wooden or plastic club-shaped objects which are targets for bowling balls*

racquetball: *a game played on a four-wall court with rackets and a rubber ball*

ramp: *a type of slide for a bowling ball that helps young children and people with disabilities to roll the ball down the alley*

regulars: *people who come to a place often*

resumed: *began again*

reunite: *get together again*

scowling: *frowning to show irritation*

shrugged: *raised shoulders in a gesture of "oh well"*

slow motion: *moving very slowly*

slowpokes: *people who move very slowly*

snazzy: *attractive; in style*

swerved: *veered away from going in a straight line*

84

techniques: *ways of doing certain physical movements (so you can bowl well)*

tournament: *sports contest involving several teams*

"way back when": *an expression meaning long ago*

winced: *made a face as if in pain*

The Power of a Girl

For every *Our Generation®* product you buy, a portion of sales goes to WE Charity's Power of a Girl Initiative to help provide girls in developing countries an education—the most powerful tool in the world for escaping poverty.

Did you know that out of the millions of children who aren't in school, 70% of them are girls? In developing communities around the world, many girls can't go to school. Usually it's because there's no school available or because their responsibilities to family (farming, earning an income, walking hours each day for water) prevent it.

WE Charity has had incredible success in its first 20 years. Together, we've built more than 1,000 school rooms, empowering more than 200,000 children with an education. As WE Charity continues to deepen its programming, it's focusing on creating sustainable communities through its holistic development model built on the five Pillars of Impact: Education, Water, Health, Food and Opportunity.

The most incredible part about this model is that roughly a quarter of WE Charity's funding comes from kids just like you, who have lemonade stands, bake sales, penny drives, walkathons and more.

Just by buying an *Our Generation* product you have helped change the world, and you are powerful (beyond belief!) to help even more.

If you want to find out more, visit:
www.ogdolls.com/we-charity

 Together we change the world.

this is **our** story®

We are an extraordinary generation of girls. And have we got a story to tell.

Our Generation® is unlike any that has come before. We're helping our families learn to recycle, holding bake sales to support charities, and holding penny drives to build homes for orphaned children in Haiti. We're helping our little sisters learn to read and even making sure the new kid at school has a place to sit in the cafeteria.

All that and we still find time to play hopscotch and hockey. To climb trees, do cartwheels all the way down the block and laugh with our friends until milk comes out of our noses. You know, to be kids.

Will we have a big impact on the world? We already have. What's ahead for us? What's ahead for the world? We have no idea. We're too busy grabbing and holding on to the joy that is today.

Yep. This is our time. This is our story.

www.ogdolls.com

Make Your Own Bowling Lane!

Everly's favorite sport is bowling—and many of the other kids in her class love it, too. What about you? Want to give it a try? You don't even need to go to the bowling alley. Instead make your own bowling lane at home. See how much fun it can be to bowl with your friends and family.

Supplies You Will Need:
10 empty plastic water or soda bottles with caps
colorful stickers or markers (if you wish to decorate the bottles)
flour or water
masking tape (for indoor game) or chalk (for outdoor game)
lightweight ball (try different sizes!)

The goal of the game is to knock down all the pins with the ball!

To Prepare the Game
1. Fill the empty bottles with enough flour or water so they do not easily fall over.
2. Choose an area for your bowling lane that measures 10 to 15 steps out from a wall and is at least 5 steps wide. Indoors, you'll need an uncarpeted floor. Outdoors you'll need a non-grassy flat area. Be sure there are no breakable items nearby.
3. Use tape or chalk to make a "foul line" 15 steps from the wall.
4. Set up the 10 bottles or "pins" in a triangular pattern, near the wall, like this:

How to Play:
1. Each player rolls the ball towards the pins without stepping over the foul line.
2. Each player has two turns in a row to knock down as many "pins" as possible. (Don't set up the pins again between these two turns.)
3. Keep track of the number of pins each player knocks down.
4. Set up the 10 pins for the next bowler.
5. When each player has bowled, play again! See who can get the highest score.

this is my favorite sports story:

About the Author

Susan Hughes is an award-winning writer of more than 30 children's books, including picture books, chapter books, young adult novels, nonfiction for all ages, and even a graphic non-fiction book. Susan is also a freelance editor who works with educational publishers to develop student books and teacher materials for a variety of grade levels. In addition, she helps coach and guide other writers in revising and polishing their own manuscripts.

About the Illustrator

Passionate about drawing from an early age, Géraldine Charette decided to pursue her studies in computer multimedia in order to further develop her style and technique. Her favorite themes to explore in her illustrations are fashion and urban life. In her free time, Géraldine loves to paint and travel. She is passionate about horses and loves spending time at the stable. It's where she feels most at peace and gives her time to think and fuel her creativity.

A Love of Bowling became the book that you are holding in your hands with the assistance of the talented people at Maison Battat Inc., including Joe Battat, Dany Battat, Véronique Chartrand, Sandy Jacinto, Loredana Ramacieri, Véronique Casavant, Ananda Guarany, Jenny Gambino, Natalie Cohen, Arlee Stewart, Karen Erlichman, Zeynep Yasar and Pam Shrimpton.